Silvana Julieta Barboni (under the pen name Selva) is an ESOL Teacher and Translator. She taught English for children, teenagers and adults in international contexts and currently works as a Senior Lecturer at the National University of La Plata, Argentina. Among her main interests is the role of education to help generate the changes required by our world today. She has written and published several children's stories and ELT books for the local context of Argentina.

Laura Fernández Saad is an artist and arts teacher and has been involved in the illustration of children's books for thirty years. She is also a lecturer in the School of Arts at the National University of Buenos Aires, Argentina. She has worked as an illustrator and designer and holds an interest in illustrating educational materials with citizenship concerns for children.

CHILDHOODS

Author:SELVA

Illustrated By: LAURA FERNÁNDEZ SAAD

AUSTIN MACAULEY PUBLISHERS™

LONDON • CAMBRIDGE • NEW YORK • SHARJAH

A CIP catalogue record for this title is available from the British Library.

ISBN 9781035847945 (Paperback)
ISBN 9781035847952 (ePub e-book)

www.austinmacauley.com

First Published 2024
Austin Macauley Publishers Ltd®
1 Canada Square
Canary Wharf
London
E14 5AA

I dedicate this book to my great grandparents, Francesco Pezza and Fermina Tozzi. My eternal gratitude and love to their mothers for whom life was the only possible choice.

I would like to thank the children in my teaching context who inspired this book.

SOME CHILDREN...

A rabbit's ears,
A turtle's shell,
A bear's muzzle,
A lizard's legs.

HAVE ALL CHOICES.

A tiger's fur,
A zebra's legs,
A lion's mane,
A fish's scales.

BUT THERE ARE OTHERS...

WHO HAVE...

NO CHOICE.

A bear's ears,
A bird's song,
A dinosaur's spikes,
A unicorn's horn.

IGNORED, LONELY AND NEGLECTED.

AT RISK, THEY LONG FOR...

CARE AND STILL DREAM...

CHILDREN'S DREAMS.

A cat's warmth,
An owl's watch,
A dog's custody,
A horse's loyalty.